ABC
BOOK OF WORDS

by Ellen Rudin and Justine Korman

Pictures by Kelly Oechsli

GOLDEN PRESS® NEW YORK

Western Publishing Company, Inc.
Racine, Wisconsin

GOLDEN FUN AT HOME WORKBOOKS™

ISBN 0-307-01461-4
EFGHIJ

ABC Book of Words

This is a book of words.

Another name for it is Dictionary.

A dictionary tells what some words mean.

In it are words you already know

and some that are new.

You can find the words you know

and also learn the new words.

In the back

there are good words to think about

like Adventure.

You can look in your ABC Book of Words

again and again.

Have fun!

A a

accident

An accident is something that happens without anyone wanting it to happen.

address

An address tells where someone lives.

adult

An adult is a full-grown person or animal.

afternoon

Afternoon is the time after lunch and before dinner.

apron

An apron protects clothes.

animals

B b

bandage

A bandage is for when you are hurt.

birthday

Your birthday comes every year on the day you were born.

blanket

A blanket keeps you warm.

bowl

A bowl holds foods that won't stay on a plate.

bubble

box

A box that is empty has many uses. A full box is sometimes a present.

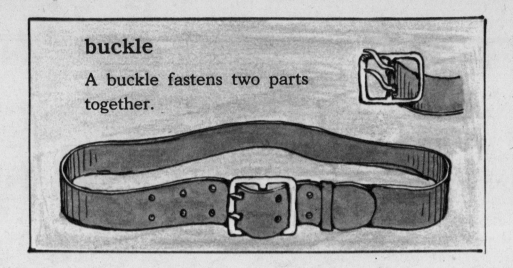

buckle

A buckle fastens two parts together.

bug

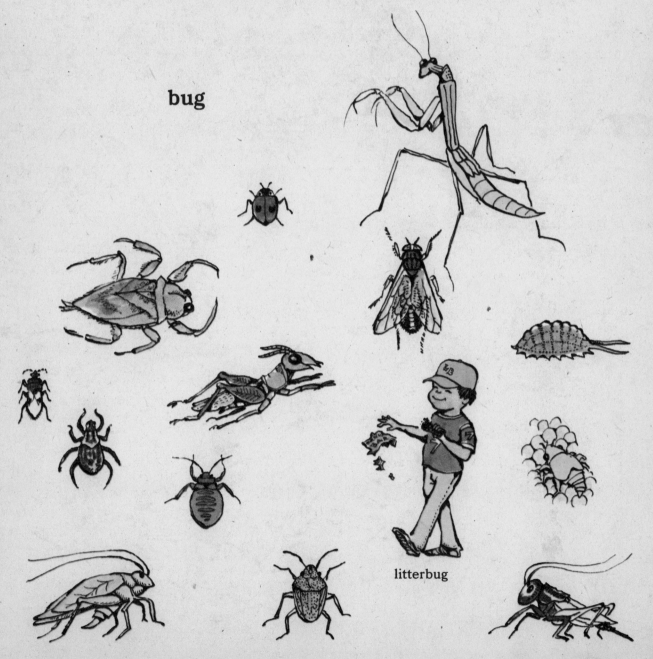

litterbug

Say the words that begin with the letter b.

boat

ball

boy

bucket

beach

butterfly

blanket

bat

brush

beak

bird

8

blimp

building

bus

bay

bike

bricks

broom

bench

barrel

boardwalk

bonnet

baby

basket

bald

beard

buns

bread

beach robe

bag

bananas

bottle

9

C c

cartoon

Cartoons in newspapers and
books are drawings.
Cartoons on television
are drawings that move.

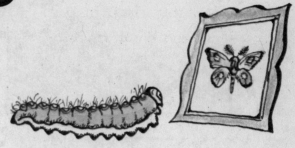

caterpillar

A caterpillar will grow up to be
a butterfly or a moth.

castle

cave

A cave is a big dark hole in the side of a hill or mountain.

closet

A closet is a place to put things away.

cloud

A cloud looks fluffy but it is made of tiny drops of water.

cracker

A cracker to eat is flat and crisp and sometimes salty.

crayon

Crayons for coloring are made of different colors of wax.

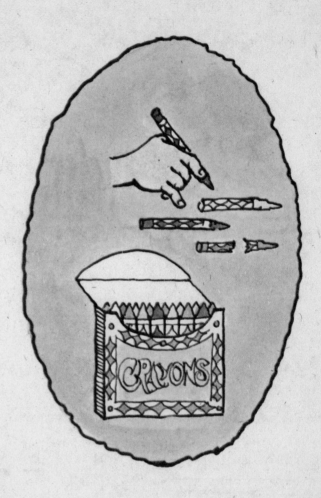

D d

dentist

A dentist takes care of teeth.

dinner

Dinner is the biggest meal of the day.

dinosaur

Dinosaurs are huge animals that lived a long time ago.

donut

A donut is a kind of fried cake.

dream

A dream can be something you want or something in your mind while you sleep.

dragon

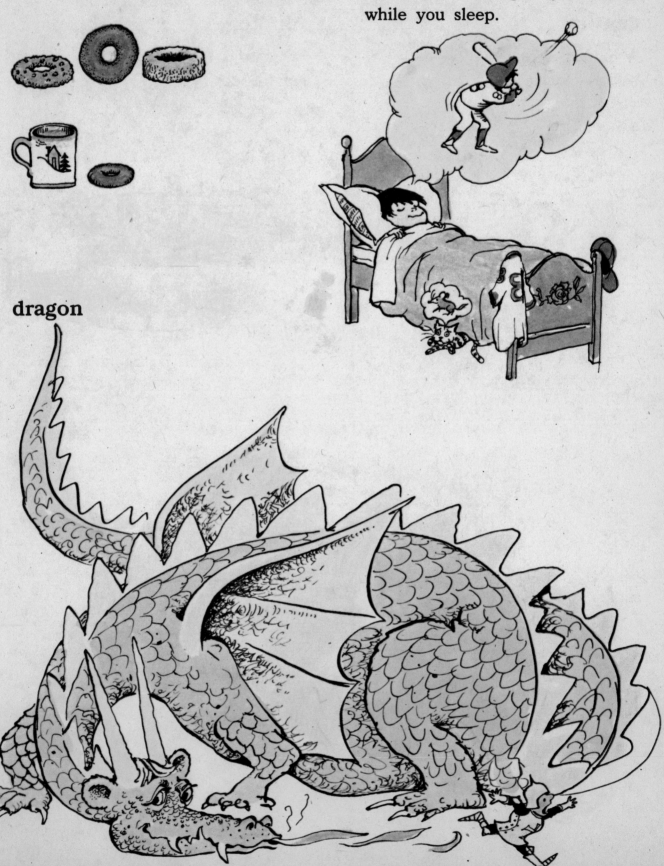

E e

echo

An echo is a sound that comes back to you.

eggshell

An eggshell is the very thin outside of an egg.

eel

An eel is a fish that looks like a snake.

elbow

elf

An elf is a small magical person in storybooks.

elevator

An elevator is a machine that carries people or things from one floor of a building to another floor.

eraser

An eraser rubs away mistakes.

F f

fever

A fever makes you feel hot and sick.

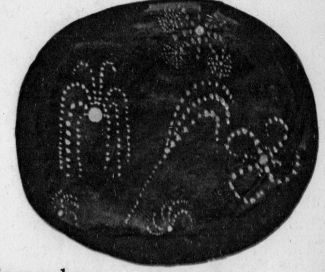

fireworks

Fireworks are a grand display of colored sparks.

fire engine

fork

fringe

A fringe goes on the end of something for decoration.

frog

A frog lives both on land and
in water.

fur

Fur is thick hair on the skin
of many animals.

G g

giant

A giant is bigger than anyone you know.

glue

Glue sticks things together.

gold

Gold is a yellow metal that is used for jewelry and money.

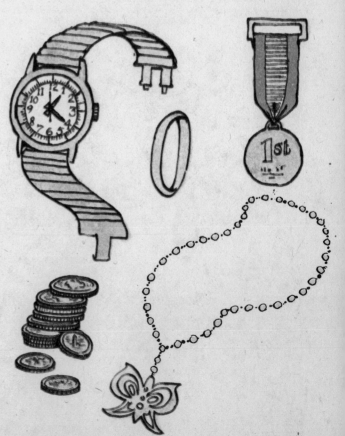

20

gorilla

A gorilla is the biggest kind
of ape.

grapes

Grapes are fruit to eat plain
or for juice or jelly.

grasshopper

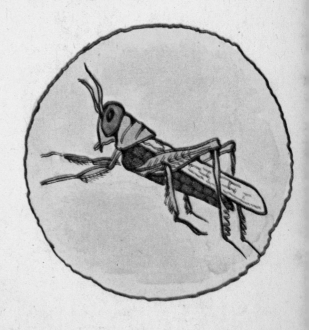

H h

hammer

A hammer is a tool for banging.

hamster

handlebars

Handlebars are used to steer bicycles and motorcycles.

home

Home is wherever you live.

hoof

A hoof is the hard foot of some animals.

hood

A hood covers your whole head.

hug

Say the words that begin with the letter h.

helicopter

hill

house

hay

hedge

hare

handle

hogs

hen

horns

hummingbird

hive

hole

hound

hat

hoe

horse

haystack

horn

I i

icicle

An icicle is dripping water that froze.

ingredient

An ingredient is one part of a whole thing.

insect

An insect is a tiny animal with six legs.
Sometimes an insect is called a bug.

island

An island is land with water all around it.

ivy

Ivy is a vine with shiny leaves that stay green all year.

J j

jacket

A jacket is a short coat.

juice

Juice can be squeezed from a fruit or a vegetable.

jewels

junk

Junk is a name for things that nobody else wants.

K k

kangaroo

Kangaroos are wild animals that live only in Australia and on the islands around it.

ketchup

Ketchup is a red sauce that tastes good with other food.

key

A key opens a lock.

kite

A kite can fly only in the wind.

kitten

A kitten is a young cat.

L l

lamp

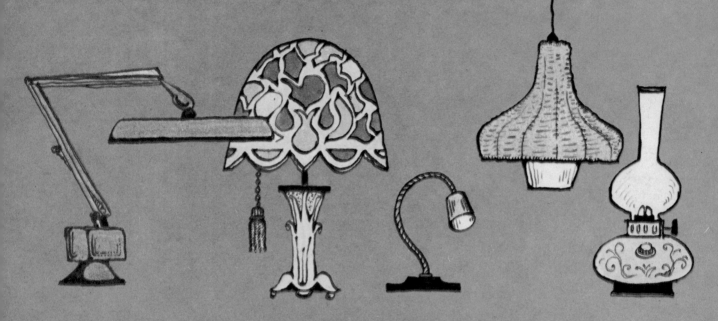

lap

A lap is the top of the thighs when a person sits down.

leftovers

Leftovers are food that was on the table but was not eaten.

leotard

A leotard is a tight suit
to wear when you exercise.

library

A library is a place that lends
books.

lion

A lion is a large wild cat.

lipstick

Lipstick is make-up for lips.

lump

A lump is a raised spot in something smooth.

M m

mailbox

A mailbox is a box for letters.

map

A map shows where places are.

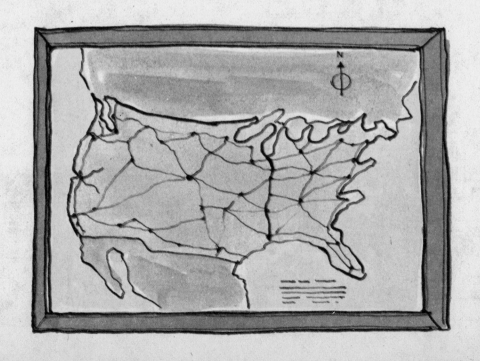

mask

A mask hides a person's face.

mop

A mop is used to clean the floor.

moon

The moon comes out at night.

morning

Morning is all the time after sunrise and before lunch.

mud

Mud is a messy mixture of dirt and water.

mustache

A mustache is the hair some men grow on their upper lips.

Say the words that begin with the letter m.

magazines

muffins

margarine

milk

meats

melons

mop

mitten

MARKET

MARKET

mayonnaise

mushrooms

maple
syrup

N n

napkin

A napkin is for wiping your mouth and fingers when you eat.

night

Night comes when the sun sets.

nest

A nest is the home of some animals.

noodle

Noodles are thin strips of cooked dough to eat in soup or with other foods.

O o

oatmeal

Oatmeal is uncooked cereal
that can be made into hot cereal
or made into oatmeal cookies.

ocean

An ocean is salt water
as far as you can see.

octopus

An octopus is a sea animal with eight arms called tentacles.

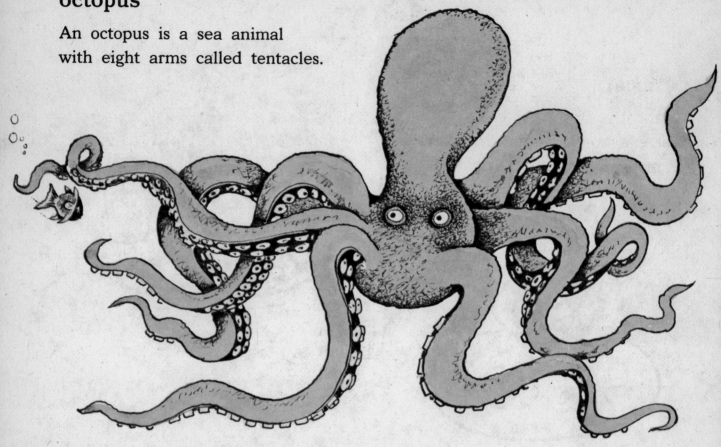

olive

Olives are extra food like pickles.

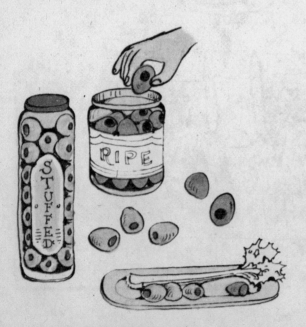

overalls

40

P p

pancake

Pancakes are a special breakfast.

paw

Paws are the soft padded feet of some animals.

picnic

A picnic is a meal people bring outside.

pillow

A pillow is something soft to lean against.

puddle

pocket

Pockets are spaces inside clothes for carrying things.

puppy

A puppy is a young dog.

Q q

queen

quintuplets

Quintuplets are five babies with the same mother and father, all born at the same time.

quilt

A quilt is a warm bed cover made from two pieces of cloth with stuffing sewn between them.

R r

raccoon

A raccoon is a small friendly animal that lives in trees and stays awake at night.

refrigerator

A refrigerator is a cabinet with a motor that keeps food cold.

rainbow

A rainbow is a hoop of colors in the sky made when the sun shines through drops of rain.

ribbon

A ribbon is a strip of pretty material for tying things.

rice

Rice is a good food made from the seeds of a kind of grass that grows in warm wet places.

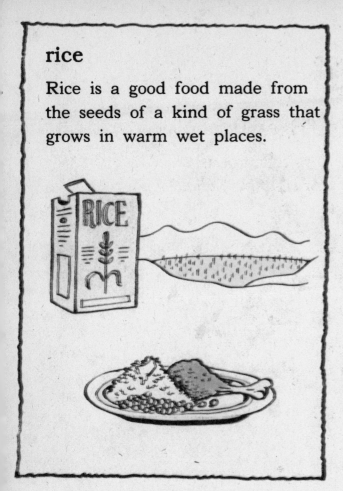

roof

A roof is the top of a building.

roller coaster

A roller coaster is a ride in an amusement park that goes up and down on very steep tracks.

45

S s

sandwich

A sandwich is two pieces of bread with something to eat between them.

scissors

Scissors are a tool with two blades for cutting.

shovel

A shovel is a scoop for lifting dirt, sand, snow, and other loose things.

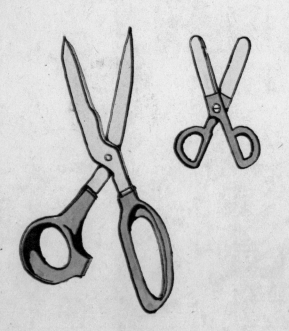

46

sidewalk

A sidewalk is a safe place to walk along a road or street.

snack

A snack is something to eat between meals.

string

String is thin rope used to tie things together.

slipper

Slippers are shoes to wear indoors.

Say the words that
begin with the letter s.

steeple

street

sign

sidewalk

schoolyard

soccer game

shadow

48

sun

sky

school

shirt

shoes

slide

irrel

socks

skirt

spoon

sweater

sand

shovel

sandbox

swings

sneakers

49

T t

tail

tent

A tent is a shelter made of cloth
or animal skin.

tire

A tire is the ring of rubber
that covers a wheel.

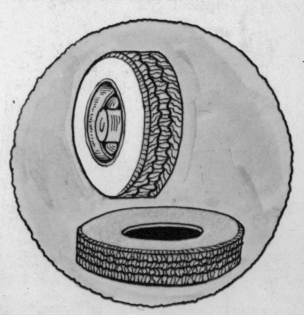

towel

typewriter

A typewriter is a machine that prints letters on paper when you tap the keys with your fingers.

turtle

Turtles can be tiny or enormous, and some live on land and some live in water.

U u

umbrella

uncle

An uncle is the brother of a person's father or mother.

underwear

Underwear is the first thing to put on when you get dressed.

V v

vase

A vase holds water and flowers.

vegetable

visitor

A visitor is someone who comes to your home to spend time with you.

volcano

A volcano is an opening in the earth that lets out steam and melted rock.

W w

waterfall

A waterfall is water that falls over a ledge of rocks into more water below.

watermelon

weeds

Weeds are plants that people don't want to grow.

whiskers

Whiskers are stiff hairs
that grow near the mouths of
some animals.

whistle

A whistle makes a high sound
when you blow through it.

worm

The worm that people see
most often is the earthworm, but
there are other kinds of worms.

X x

There are very few words in the English language that begin with the letter x.

x-ray

An x-ray is a special kind of photograph that shows the insides of people or things.

xylophone

A xylophone is a musical instrument that is played with wooden hammers.

Y y

yam

A yam is a big, sweet, orange potato.

yolk

The yolk is the yellow part of an egg.

yogurt

Yogurt is a smooth food made from milk that can be a snack or a meal.

yo-yo

A yo-yo is a toy that goes up and down on a string tied to your finger.

Z z

zebra

zip code

A zip code is a group of numbers at the end of an address.

zero

A zero stands for none or nothing.

zipper

A zipper is used to zip two sides together.

Here are some words to think about.

A a

adventure

B b

beach

beehive

blossom

C c

camping

canoe

D d

deer

diamond

dragonfly

E e

emergency

F f

feather
flavor
forest

G g

garden
ghost
gift
giraffe

H h

hiccup
hide-and-seek

I i

idea
imagination
invention

J j

jellyfish
joke
joy

K k

kaleidoscope
king
kiss
kitchen

L l

land
language
leader
lightning

M m

machine
make-believe
meadow

N n

name
noise
noose

O o

odor
onion
opinion
orchestra
owner

P p

paddle
palace
pest
plan

Q q

quantity
question

R r

race
reason
rose

S s

sailor
science
seashore
shadow
star
storm

T t

team
thunder
time
treasure
trip

U u

universe

V v

vacuum
  cleaner
victory
vitamin
voice
voyage

W w

wave
whale
wilderness
wind
wings

X x

Xerox machine

Y y

year
yesterday
you
young

Z z

zephyr
zest
zigzag